Copyright © 1997 by Ken Brown
All rights reserved.
CIP Data is available.
Published in the United States 1997 by Dutton Children's Books,
a division of Penguin Books USA Inc.
375 Hudson Street, New York, New York 10014

Originally published in Great Britain 1997 by Andersen Press, Ltd, London
Typography by Richard Amari
First American Edition
Printed in Italy     ISBN 0-525-45886-7
2 4 6 8 10 9 7 5 3 1

# Mucky Pup

**Ken Brown**

*Dutton Children's Books*

N E W   Y O R K

The new puppy was having a wonderful time.
He emptied the trash can, cleaned out the coal bucket,

rearranged the tablecloth, and shook the cushions—what fun!

But the farmer's wife didn't think the mess was much fun at all. "You're a good-for-nothing mucky pup!" she scolded. "Out you go!"

Mucky Pup didn't know what to make of his
new name. He trotted out to the barnyard
to find someone who wanted to play.

"Will you play with me?" he asked the rooster,
who was preening his long, beautiful tail feathers.

"*Cock-a-doodle*-don't be stupid," crowed the rooster.
"I am king of the henhouse—you're nothing
but a mucky pup."

So Mucky Pup ambled down to the duck pond.
"Will you play with me?" he asked one of the
little yellow ducklings who paddled near the bank.

"You must be *quack, quack,* quackers!"
quacked the duckling. "I'm a champion swimmer—
you're nothing but a mucky pup."

So Mucky Pup wandered into the cool, shady barn.
"Will you play with me?" he asked the marmalade cat
who was stretched out on a bag of grain.
   "How *purrr*fectly ridiculous," purred the handsome cat.
"I'm a fearless mouser—you're nothing but a mucky pup."

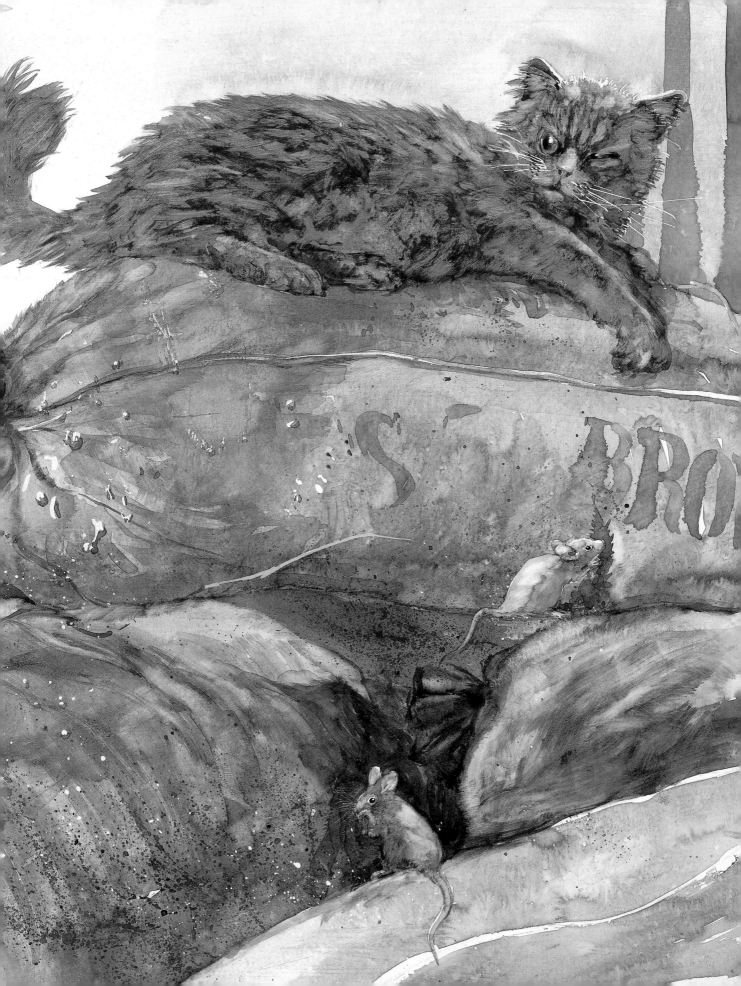

Mucky Pup scrambled up on a hay bale, and asked the horse, "Will you play with me, please? Please?"

"*Naaay*, nay," neighed the huge horse. "I'm a magnificent shire-horse—you're nothing but a mucky pup."

Mucky Pup felt very lonely. Wouldn't anyone play with him?

Maybe the other animals were right after all— he was just too mucky.

He wandered sadly outside into the yard.

Suddenly a snout appeared through the slats of the gate.
"Hello," said a very muddy piglet. "Will you play with me?"
"No," the puppy said miserably. "I'm just a mucky pup."
"But I'm just a mucky pig," said the piglet. "Let's play in the
mucky mud!"

And that's just what they did—until . . .

"Here, pup! Mucky pup!" called the farmer's wife. "Bath time!"
But mucky pup didn't need a bath.

His fur was clean and soft again, and his busy day had made him very sleepy. He settled down by the fire to dream about what fun it was to be nothing but a **mucky pup.**